alphabet mystery

Aa Bb Cc Dd

Ee Ff Gg Hh Ii

Jj Kk Ll Mm Nn

Oo Pp Qq Rr Ss

Tt Uu Vv Ww

Xx Yy Zz

alphabet
mystery

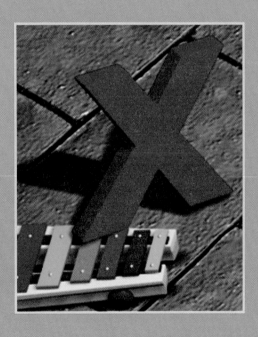

by **AUDREY WOOD**
illustrated by **BRUCE WOOD**

SCHOLASTIC INC.
New York Toronto London Auckland Sydney
Mexico City New Delhi Hong Kong Buenos Aires

This book was originally published in hardcover by the Blue Sky Press in 2003.

ISBN 0-439-68363-7

12 11 10   5 6 7 8 9/0

Printed in the U.S.A.   40

The illustrations in this book were created digitally using
various 3-D modeling software packages, assisted by Adobe Photoshop.

First Scholastic paperback printing, September 2004

For my mom, Audrey Wood—B.W.

Every night, the little letters from Charley's Alphabet tuck themselves into bed. And every night, just for fun, each one calls out his name.

"a-b-c-d-e-f-g-h-i-j-k-l-m-n-o-p-q-r-s-t-u-v-w-y-z!"
But tonight, something is wrong. Who didn't say his name?

"Little **x** is absent!" Little **a** exclaimed.

"I'm shocked!" said Little **i**. "One of Charley's pencils is gone, too."

"This is terrible!" Little **t** said. "I think Little **x** took a pencil and flew away."
"But why did he do it?" Little **d** asked. "We must go find Little **x** and solve this mystery."

Charley's Alphabet jumped aboard another
pencil and took off across the night sky.

They zoomed over cities, towns,
and fields, looking for their friend.

"Stop!" Little **s** shouted. "I spy one of Charley's pencils parked at the castle below us."

When they landed, a heavy door creaked open. In a voice as creaky as the door, a crooked Capital **I** said, "Who dares to visit the Master's castle in the middle of the night?" Brave Little **b** spoke up:

"We've come to solve a mystery. Have you seen Little **x**?"
"Follow me," Crooked *I* said, "but don't wake the Master,
or you'll be alphabet soup!"

Charley's Alphabet tiptoed across the floor of the castle library. A gigantic Capital **M** was asleep at a huge table.

And, much to their surprise, there was Little **x**,
tap-dancing a lullaby on a xylophone!

Quick as winks, they jumped to the tabletop and hurried over to Little **x**.
"We've come to rescue you," Little **r** said. "Let's get out of here. Run!"

"I don't want to go," Little **x** said, as he continued to dance.
"I ran away because Charley never uses me. A Little **x** is just
a worthless letter back home. At least here I have a job."

"I know a secret," Little **i** said. "Charley wants to give his mother a special present for her birthday tomorrow. He plans to use you more than any of us!"

Little **x** was so surprised he stopped dancing on the xylophone . . .

. . . and that's when the giant **M** awakened.

"MMMM!" **M** said. "I see little letters! Fire up the pot,
Crooked *I*. It's time for alphabet soup!" All of the little
letters began to tremble.

Little **x** knew he had made a terrible mistake running away
from his alphabet family. He had to think fast.
"Master **M**!" he said. "Do you know what *M* stands for?"

Giant **M** bent down low. "Mad, miserable monster!" he said.
"Now get back to work, or I'll throw you in the pot, too!"

"M also stands for *mother*," clever Little **x** continued.
"Charley's mother is having a birthday, and he needs all
of us for her special surprise. You don't want his mother
to have an unhappy birthday, do you?"

Suddenly Giant **M** burst out crying. "I have a mother, too," he said, "but I haven't given her a special surprise in so long. We should show our mothers how much we care, no matter how big we grow."

Opening the door to his treasure room, Giant **M** said through his tears, "I want Charley's mother to have the best birthday ever.

So each of you can choose a gift for her. Then you may go home."
Which present did each letter choose?

Little **x** invited Crooked *I* and Giant **M** to the birthday party.

Just as the sun was rising, they all blasted off for home on the pencils.

That morning, Charley helped his dad make a cake.

Then he called for his alphabet.

Working together with their new friends, the letters jumped
on the birthday cake and made their very first sentence.

All the little letters were very proud, but Little **x** was the proudest. For the grand finishing touch, Charley used him four times. Do you know why?

Because Little **x** is the only letter in the alphabet that stands for . . .
KISSES!

Aa Bb Cc Dd
Ee Ff Gg Hh Ii
Jj Kk Ll Mm Nn
Oo Pp Qq Rr Ss
Tt Uu Vv Ww
X Yy Zz